F 101 Penworthy

D1402324

A Note to Parents and Teachers

The *Dorling Kindersley Readers* series is a reading program for children that is highly respected by teachers and educators around the world. The LEGO Group has a global reputation for offering high quality, innovative products, specially designed to stimulate a child's creativity and development through play.

Now Dorling Kindersley has joined forces with The LEGO Group, to produce the first-ever graded reading program to be based around LEGO play themes. Each *Dorling Kindersley Reader* is guaranteed to capture a child's imagination, while developing his or her reading skills, general knowledge, and love of reading.

The books are written and designed in conjunction with leading literacy experts, including Dr. Linda Gambrell, Director of the School of Education at Clemson University. Dr. Gambrell has served on the Board of Directors of the International Reading Association and as President of the National Reading Conference.

The four levels of *Dorling Kindersley Readers* are aimed at different reading abilities, enabling you to choose the books that are right for each child.

Level 1 – Beginning to Read
Level 2 – Beginning to Read Alone
Level 3 – Reading Alone
Level 4 – Proficient Readers

The "normal" age at which a child begins to read can be anywhere from three to eight years old, so these levels are only guidelines.

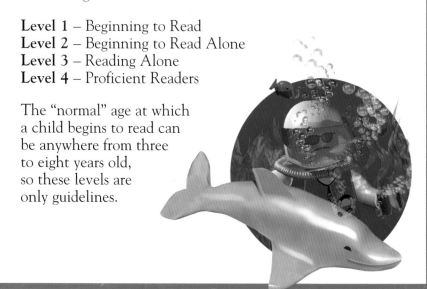

Dorling DK Kindersley

LONDON, NEW YORK, SYDNEY, DELHI, PARIS,
MUNICH, and JOHANNESBURG

Senior Editor Cynthia O'Neill
Senior Art Editor Nick Avery
Senior Managing Art Editor Cathy Tincknell
DTP Designer Andrew O'Brien
Production Nicola Torode
US Editor Gary Werner

Reading Consultant Linda Gambrell, PhD

First American Edition, 2000

00 01 02 03 04 05 10 9 8 7 6 5 4 3 2 1

Published in the United States by
Dorling Kindersley Publishing, Inc.
95 Madison Avenue
New York, New York 10016

Dorling Kindersley books are available at special discounts for bulk
purchases for sales promotions or premiums. Special editions,
including personalized covers, excerpts of existing guides, and
corporate imprints can be created in large quantities for specific
needs. For more information, contact Special Markets Dept./
Dorling Kindersley Publishing, Inc./95 Madison Ave./New York,
NY 10016/ Fax:800-600-9098

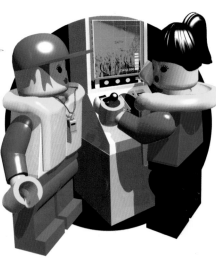

Library of Congress Cataloging-in-Publication Data
Birkinshaw, Marie.
    Secret at Dolphin Bay / by Marie Birkinshaw.-- 1st American ed.
    p. cm. -- (Dorling Kindersley LEGO readers)
    Summary: Fay Fixit, Steve Spanner, and Lifeguard Sally hurry to
Dolphin Bay where Tessa the sea veterinarian is stranded with an
injured dolphin.
    ISBN 0-7894-6699-6 -(hc)- ISBN 0-7894-6700-3 (pbk)
    [1. Dolphins--Fiction. 2. Bays--Fiction.] I. Title. II. Series.
PZ7.B5225 Se 2000
[E]--dc21
                                00-024011
Printed in China by L Rex

see our complete
catalog at
www.dk.com

DORLING KINDERSLEY *READERS* LEGO

Secret at
Dolphin Bay

Written by Marie Birkinshaw • Illustrated by Jason Cook

BEGINNING **1** TO READ

A Dorling Kindersley Book

Fay Fixit and Steve Spanner were busy repairing Lifeguard Sally's truck.

Steve tested the brakes and Fay put some oil in the engine.

"Thanks for your help!"
said Sally.
"Now I must get back to work.
This afternoon, we're testing
the new rescue boat."

"Can we come with you?"
asked Steve.
"We aren't very busy today,"
Fay told Sally.

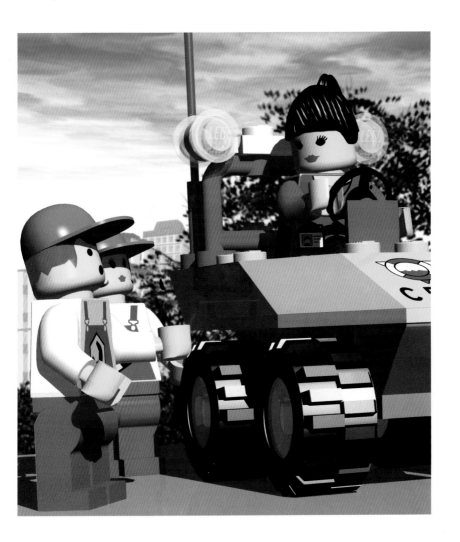

At the harbor,
Steve and Fay helped Diver Dan
push the boat into the water.

Then the friends climbed
on board the boat.
"Let's go!" said Sally.

On the boat deck
was a box of new tools.
"I wish we could test these tools!"
Steve joked to Fay.

Suddenly, the alarm sounded.
Eee-ohh! Eee-ohh!

Sally called back to base and
talked to the coast guard.
Then she spoke to her friends.
"A dinghy is in trouble," she said.
"We must go to Dolphin Bay!"

At Dolphin Bay,
Tessa the sea vet
was waiting for help.

"I came to help a dolphin
who had cut his flipper,"
said Tessa.
"But now my boat won't start!"

"Don't worry," Fay told Tessa. "We've been looking forward to testing the new tools!"

"We'll be busy too,"
Lifeguard Sally said to Dan.
"We must find out
how the dolphin cut his flipper."

"I think there's some sharp metal
hidden under the water,"
said Tessa.
"I'll try to find it
with the underwater camera,"
Sally told her.

"I'll dive down and look too," said Diver Dan.

Dan jumped into the sea.
Some rainbow fish followed him
as he swam around,
looking for the sharp metal.

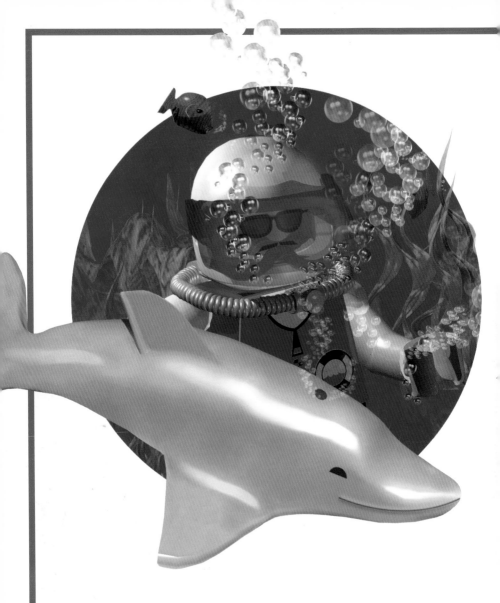

Then the dolphin swam up to Dan.
He tapped Dan's arm
with his nose!
Then he swam away.

"Maybe the dolphin
wants me to follow him,"
thought Dan.
So he swam after the dolphin.

Fay and Steve had repaired
Tessa's boat.
"Thank you so much,"
said Tessa.

Then Diver Dan
came back to the surface.
"The dolphin has led me
to a metal box," he said.
"It has very sharp sides.
Let's pull it out of the sea."

Everyone helped to pull
the metal box from the water.
It was very heavy.

Dan opened the box carefully.
What a surprise!
The box was full of treasure!
"I wonder if this is stolen?"
said Sally.

27

Back at LEGO City harbor,
the police were waiting.

They looked at the treasure.
"This is gold from the castle,"
they said.
"A robber stole it long ago, and
now we can take it back."

But when the harbor police
tried to leave,
their boat wouldn't start.

"Let's get to work!"
Steve said to Fay.
"Time to test those tools again!"

What do they do?

Mechanics

fix broken-down
machines.

Lifeguards

help keep swimmers
and sailors safe.

Harbor
police

keep law and order
out at sea.

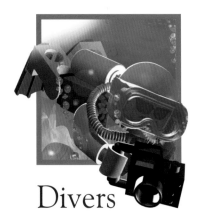

Divers

swim underwater
and explore the sea.